Hopscotch

First published in 2009
by Wayland

Text copyright © Anna Matthew
Illustration copyright © Heather Heyworth

Wayland
338 Euston Road
London NW1 3BH

Wayland Australia
Level 17/207 Kent Street
Sydney, NSW 2000

Series Editor: Louise John
Editor: Katie Powell
Cover design: Paul Cherrill
Design: D.R.ink
Consultant: Shirley Bickler

A CIP catalogue record for this book is available from the British Library.

ISBN 9780750259286

Printed in China

Wayland is a division of Hachette Children's Books,
an Hachette UK Company

www.hachette.co.uk

Hopscotch

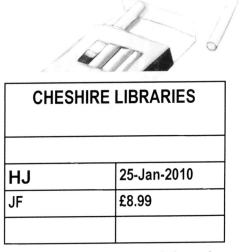

Written by Anna Matthew
Illustrated by Heather Heyworth

WAYLAND

"We want to play hopscotch," said Tom and Anna.
"One hop, two hop, three hop, four."

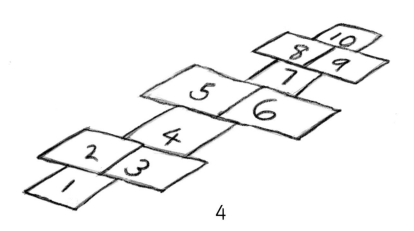

Tom and Anna want to play hopscotch in the playground.

"We can't play here," said Mum. "The playground is full."

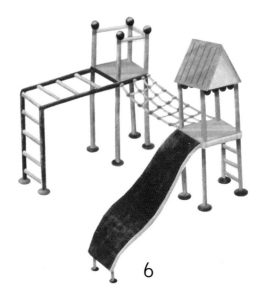

Tom and Anna want
to play hopscotch in
the park.

"The park is shut,"
said Anna. "We can't
play here."

"We can play hopscotch in the garden," said Mum.

Tom and Anna play
hopscotch in the garden.

"One hop, two hop,
three hop, four," said
Tom and Anna.

"Here comes the rain!"
said Anna.

"We can't play hopscotch
in the rain," said Tom.

"We can't play hopscotch at all!" said Anna.

"Yes, we can," said Mum.
"We can play hopscotch
in the house!"

Tom and Anna play hopscotch in the house.

"One hop, two hop, three hop, four. One hop, two hop, three hop, more!" said Tom and Anna.

Guiding a First Read of
Hopscotch

It is important to talk through the book with the child before they read it alone. This prepares them for the way the story unfolds, and allows them to enjoy the pictures as you both talk naturally, using the language they will later encounter when reading. Read them the brief overview below, and then follow the suggestions:

1. Talking through the book
Tom and Anna want to play hopscotch,
but they can't find a good place to play.
Mum has the answer.

Let's read the title: **Hopscotch**
Turn to page 4. Here are Tom and Anna.
They have a little hopscotch song.
"One hop, two hop, three hop, four."
Can you sing it?
Now turn to page 6. Can they play hopscotch
in the playground? No, it's full.
What about in the park? No, it's shut.

Continue through the book, guiding the discussion to fit the text, as the child looks at the illustrations.

On page 16, Anna is fed up. "We can't play hopscotch at all," she says. But Mum has a good idea. And on page 20 they add some more to their song.

2. A first reading of the book

Ask the child to read the book independently, pointing carefully under each word (tracking) while thinking about the story. Praise attempts by the child to correct themselves, and prompt them to use their letter knowledge, the punctuation and check the meaning, for example:

> **Yes, that word looks like 'can' but check the end. That's it – 'can't'. Now reread it. Does 'can't' make sense?**

> **Did you notice those speech marks? Try it again, and make it sound like Anna talking.**

3. Follow-up activities

The high frequency words in this title are:

and can't four here in is one play said the three to two want we

- Select two high frequency words, and ask the child or group to find them throughout the book. Discuss the shape of the letters and the letter sounds.
- To memorise the words, ask the child to write them in the air, then write them repeatedly on a whiteboard or on paper, leaving a space between each attempt.

4. Encourage

- Reading the book again – with expression.
- Drawing a picture based on the story.
- Writing one or two sentences using the practised words.

23

START READING is a series of highly enjoyable books for beginner readers. **The books have been carefully graded to match the Book Bands widely used in schools.** This enables readers to be sure they choose books that match their own reading ability.

Look out for the Band colour on the book in our Start Reading logo.

The Bands are:

Pink Band 1A & 1B

Red Band 2

Yellow Band 3

Blue Band 4

Green Band 5

Orange Band 6

Turquoise Band 7

Purple Band 8

Gold Band 9

START READING books can be read independently or shared with an adult. They promote the enjoyment of reading through satisfying stories supported by fun illustrations.

Anna Matthew loves writing stories about when she was a child. She lived in a seaside town and spent lots of time playing on the beach, and in the park and street. Now her two children are growing up, and she can write about their fun and games, too!

Heather Heyworth lives in Suffolk with her husband, two children and a very demanding cat called Wooster!